Megan McDonald

is the author of the popular Judy Moody and Stink series. She says, "Once, while I was visiting a class, the kids chanted, 'Stink! Stink! Stink!' as I entered the room. In that moment, I knew that Stink had to have a series all his own." Megan McDonald lives in California.

Peter H. Reynolds

is the illustrator of all the Judy Moody and Stink books. He says, "Stink reminds me of myself growing up: dealing with a sister prone to teasing and bossing around – and having to get creative in order to stand tall beside her." Peter H. Reynolds lives in Massachusetts.

Stin

Megan McDonald

illustrated by

Peter H. Reynolds

WALKER
BOOKS

Books by Megan McDonald and Peter H. Reynolds

Judy Moody
Judy Moody Gets Famous!
Judy Moody Saves the World!
Judy Moody Predicts the Future
Judy Moody: The Doctor Is In!
Judy Moody Declares Independence!
Judy Moody: Around the World in 8½ Days
Judy Moody Goes to College
Judy Moody, Girl Detective
Judy Moody and the NOT Bummer Summer
Judy Moody and the Bad Luck Charm
Judy Moody, Mood Martian
Judy Moody and the Bucket List
Stink: The Incredible Shrinking Kid
Stink and the Incredible Super-Galactic Jawbreaker
Stink and the World's Worst Super-Stinky Sneakers
Stink and the Great Guinea Pig Express
Stink: Solar System Superhero
Stink and the Ultimate Thumb-Wrestling Smackdown
Stink and the Midnight Zombie Walk
Stink and the Freaky Frog Freakout
Stink and the Shark Sleepover
Stink-O-Pedia: Super Stink-y Stuff from A to Zzzzz
Stink-O-Pedia 2: More Stink-y Stuff from A to Z
Judy Moody & Stink: The Holly Joliday
Judy Moody & Stink: The Mad, Mad, Mad, Mad Treasure Hunt
Judy Moody & Stink: The Big Bad Blackout

Books by Megan McDonald

The Sisters Club • *The Sisters Club: Rule of Three*
The Sisters Club: Cloudy with a Chance of Boys

Books by Peter H. Reynolds

The Dot • *Ish* • *So Few of Me* • *Sky Colour*

This book is dedicated to
Rachel, Luke, and Cash Weller
M. M.

Dedicated to Michelle Sawin Kousidis,
who is an amazing "drama" director and
a very special cast member in my life!
P. H. R.

This is a work of fiction. Names, characters, places and incidents are either the product of the author's imagination or, if real, used fictitiously. All statements, activities, stunts, descriptions, information and material of any other kind contained herein are included for entertainment purposes only and should not be relied on for accuracy or replicated as they may result in injury.

Special thanks to Amanda Giguere, director of outreach for the Colorado Shakespeare Festival, for background, information, and funny stories about the Shakespeare's Sprites summer camp for ages 6 through 9.

First published in 2018 by Walker Books Ltd
87 Vauxhall Walk, London SE11 5HJ

2 4 6 8 10 9 7 5 3 1

This book has been typeset in Stone Informal

Printed and bound by CPI Group (UK) Ltd, Croydon CR0 4YY

British Library Cataloguing in Publication Data:
a catalogue record for this book is available from the British Library

ISBN 978-1-4063-7930-3

www.stinkmoody.com
www.walker.co.uk

CONTENTS

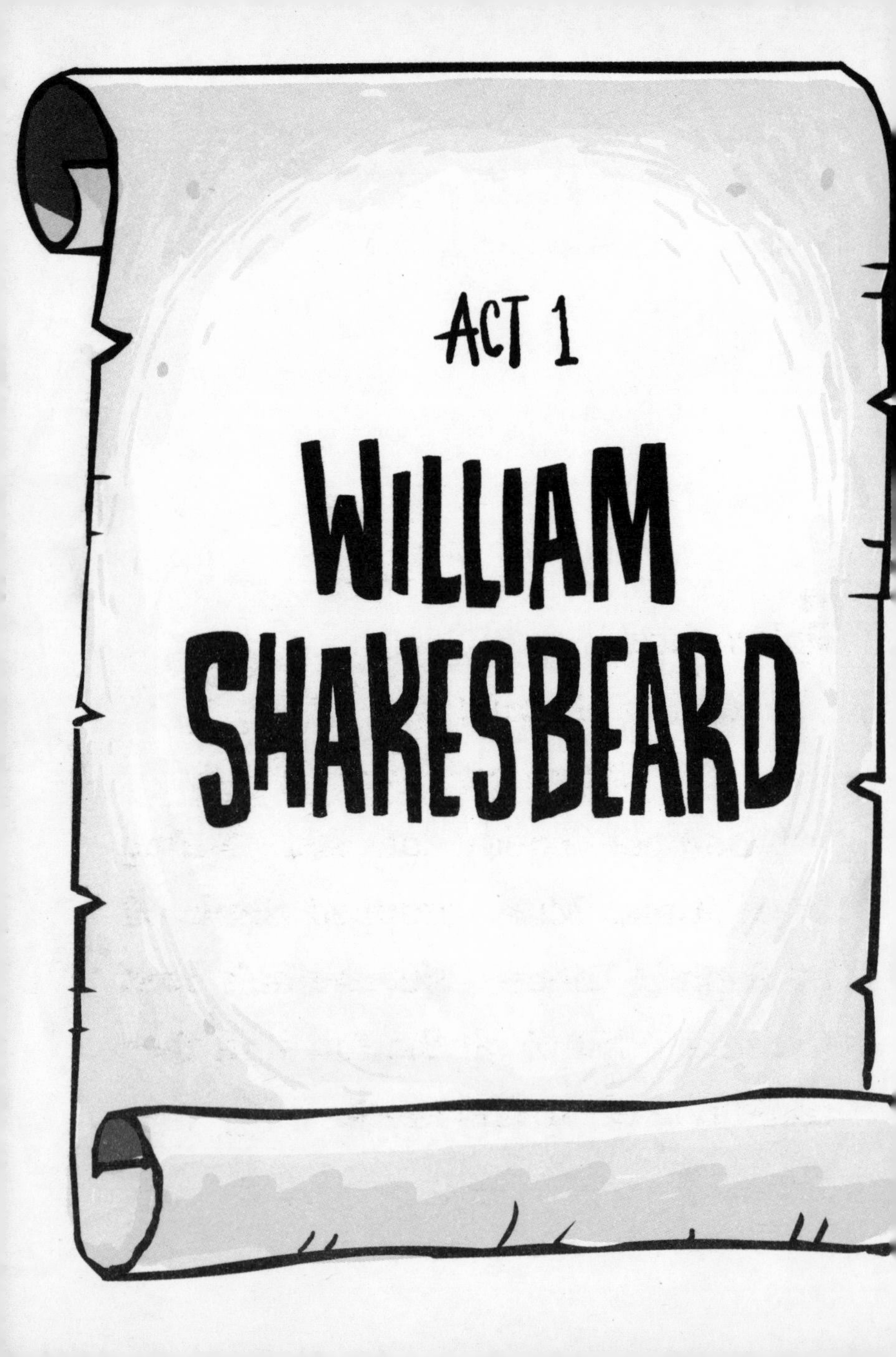

Act 1

William Shakesbeard

Spleen face!

Canker blossom!

Maggot pie!

Woo-hoo! Friday at last. Spring break time. Mum dropped Stink off at Sophie's house. He couldn't wait to make a list of all the fun stuff they could do over spring break.

Stink rang the bell. Mrs Woof let him in. He ran downstairs to the play-room. The floor was littered with flying fairies and winged horses and pointy-hatted elves. Sophie of the Elves sat smack-dab in the middle of it all.

"What's all this?" Stink asked.

Sophie held up a bag of unicorns mixed with action figures. "Look at all this good stuff I found at a yard sale!" she said. "Want to play Last Unicorn on Earth?"

Stink picked up a unicorn. "Hey, this one is missing a leg. And a bunch of them are missing horns."

Dream Big

"You just have to love them for who they are," Sophie said.

"Wait. How did a Lady-in-Her-Bathrobe toy get in here?"

"Isn't the wacky cat lady awesome? There's more, too. Moustache Guy. And Scary Dead Guy. Here's the best one." She held up a balding guy with a big collar and puffy pumpkin trousers.

"Hey, isn't that...? It's William Shakesbeard!"

Sophie cracked up. "Close! It's William Shake*speare*."

"That's what I said," said Stink. "He's that four-hundred-year-old guy who wrote all those plays, right? Webster gave me comic books of his stories. One story has a floating head in it. And a talking ghost."

"Some of his plays have fairies," said Sophie of the Elves. "And fairy queens. And kings of fairies. And elves. Ooh, I can't wait for camp."

"Camp? You're going to camp? It's not even summer."

"I'm going to Shakespeare camp for spring break. It starts Monday at the college. It's called Shakespeare Sprites. You get to dress up and act out plays, and some of the plays have sprites. You should ask your parents to sign you up, Stink, if it's not too late."

"Sprite? You get to drink soda at camp?"

"Not that kind of sprite. A sprite is a magical being, like an elf. Or a fairy."

"But I don't really want to be in a play. I'd probably get stuck being a mouse. Because I'm short, all I ever get are squeaking parts, not speaking parts."

"This camp is different. Everybody gets a speaking part."

"For real?"

"Yup. Also, there's magic and mad kings and murders in Shakespeare," said Sophie. "And storms and shipwrecks and sword fights."

Shipwrecks! Sword fights! Stink perked up. Shipwrecks and sword fights sounded way-NOT-boring.

Sophie held up the Shakespeare action figure and made him talk in a deep voice. "C'mon, Stink. Don't be a cold-blooded, vulture-headed eyeball."

"Huh?"

Sophie jumped up, and Shakespeare dropped his quill pen. "I almost forgot to tell you the best part. At Shakespeare camp, you get to swear."

Stink could not believe his ears. "No way," he said.

"Actually, it's more like funny insults. They teach you to talk like people did in Shakespeare's time. We get to have insult contests and call people silly names like 'toad-spotted bum bailey.'"

Stink cracked up. Shipwrecks and sword fights, and bum baileys and beard-wearing at college?

"So you'll come?" asked Sophie of the Elves.

"I will," said Stink.

"Did I mention you get a free T-shirt?"

Stupefying! Hie thee hither!

"TO BE, OR NOT TO BE; THAT IS THE QUESTION." —HAMLET

"ALL THE WORLD'S A STAGE." —AS YOU LIKE IT

"HE HAS NOT SO MUCH BRAIN AS EAR-WAX." —TROILUS and CRESSIDA

"BE NOT AFRAID OF GREATNESS. SOME ARE BORN GREAT." —TWELFTH NIGHT

"LORD, WHAT FOOLS THESE MORTALS BE!" —A MIDSUMMER NIGHT'S DREAM

"PARTING IS SUCH SWEET SORROW." —ROMEO and JULIET

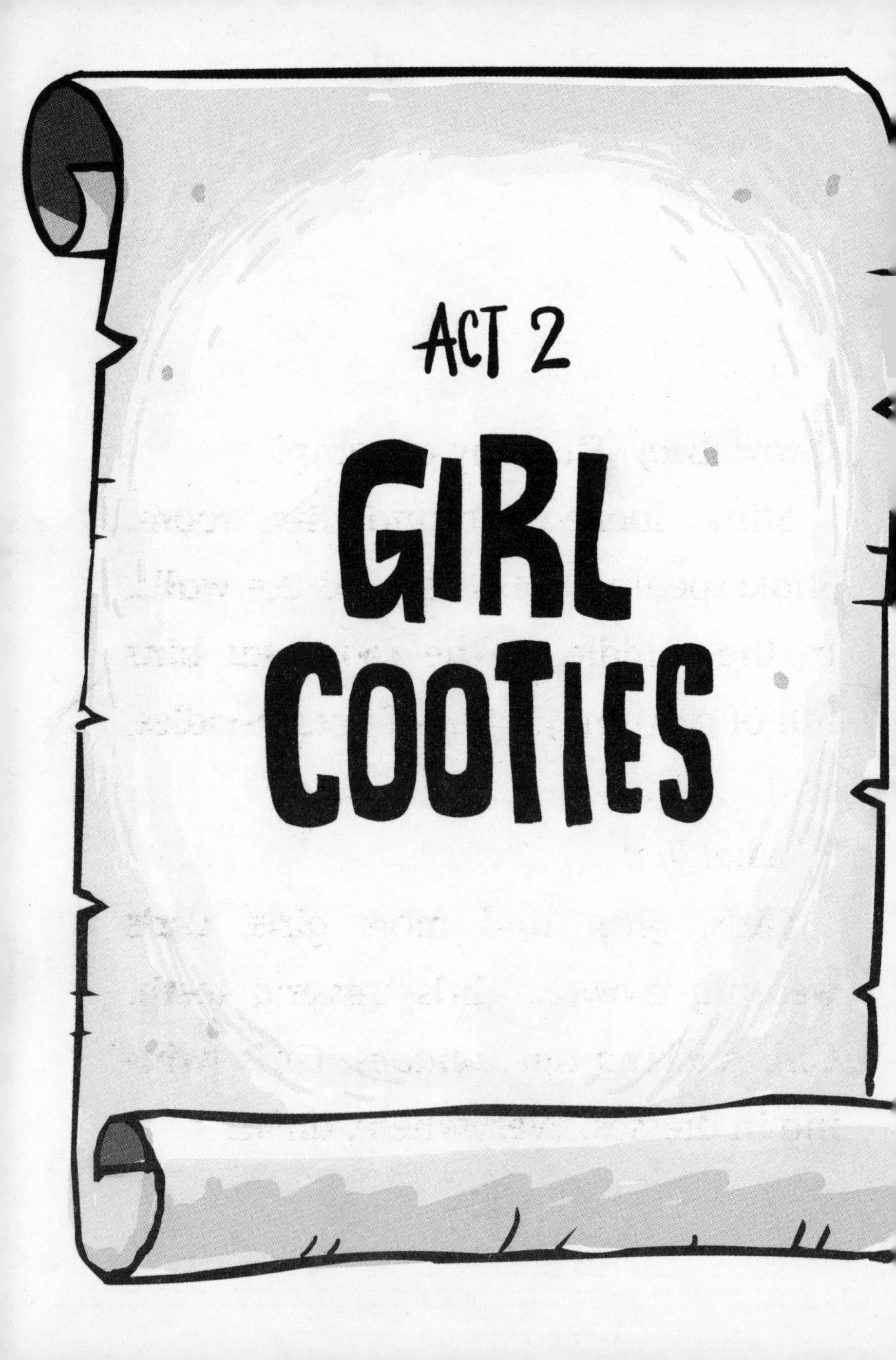

ACT 2

GIRL COOTIES

Away! Away! First day of camp!

Stink looked around the room. Shakespeare quotes covered the walls. In the middle of the room sat bins full of costumes, piles of pool noodles, and ... girls!

What, ho!

Girls, girls, and more girls. Girls wearing crowns. Girls missing teeth. Girls sticking out tongues. Girls twirling in dresses. Everywhere, girls!

to thine own self be true
To Be or Not to Be _W.S.
ALL THE WORLD'S A STAGE. - AS YOU LIKE IT
If music be the food of love- PLAY ON!
Suspicion Always
PROPS
COSTUMES

"Where are all the boys?" Stink asked Sophie.

"Huh?"

"You didn't tell me I'd be the only boy here! I'm going home."

"Hey, I counted frogs with you, Stink. I went on a midnight zombie walk with you."

"But you *liked* doing all that stuff," said Stink.

Sophie had stopped listening. She'd spotted the costumes. "Fairy wings!" she said, dashing over to the bin.

If only Webster had not gone to Mexico for spring break.

One of the millions of girls ran over to Stink. She had a crown on her head and a veil covering her face. The girl flung back the veil. *Yikes-a-roni!* Riley Rottenberger: sometimes friend, most times enemy. "What are *you* doing here?" Stink asked.

"I'm here for Shakespeare camp, same as you," said Riley.

Oh, brother. Could this day get any worse?

Just then, the acting teacher blinked the lights. "Welcome to Shakespeare Sprites! Hi, everybody! I'm Amanda Beth."

Stink plunked himself down beside Sophie. Riley scooted over next to Stink.

Amanda Beth told them all about Mr Shakespeare: that he lived in England more than four hundred years ago, that he wore a gold hoop earring, and that he knew 25,000 words. Some said he was the best writer who ever lived. "We'll also learn what it takes to be good actors," she told them.

"Do we get to be in a play?" asked a girl named Lily.

"You'll all get to act out one short scene by the end of the week," said Amanda Beth. "On Wednesday we're going to learn about a play called *Macbeth*."

"The one with the witches?" asked a girl named Harper.

"I'll be a witch!" said Hazel, a girl next to Harper.

"I'd rather be Juliet," said Riley, looking straight at Stink.

"On Wednesday night, we'll come back to campus to see real actors in an outdoor performance of *Macbeth*. On Thursday, two of the actors will visit camp to teach us swordplay."

Swordplay! Stink sat up on his heels.

"By Friday we'll be doing a dress rehearsal. Finally, on Saturday your families are invited to come watch you act out your short scenes. That's what the week looks like. Anyway, I'm glad to see so many girls—"

"Stink's the only boy!" yelled Riley. Stink's face turned cherry-popsicle red.

"In Shakespeare's time," said Amanda Beth, "it was against the law for girls to act in plays." The girls gasped. "So boys had to play all the girl parts."

"Boys wore long fancy dresses?" asked Sophie. "And princess hats?"

"They sure did. They even wore makeup and wigs."

"But since we have lots of girls, girls can play boy parts, right?" asked Sophie.

"Right," said Amanda Beth. "For an actor, that's an extra challenge. And there are no laws here like the ones in Shakespeare's time."

"I want to be a sprite," said Sophie. "Or any kind of fairy. Even a bad one."

"I'm sure everyone will get to try out a part they like."

Amanda Beth taught them how to make faces: sad faces, mad faces, glad faces. Stink practiced his best

cuckoo-crazy face on Riley.

Riley made fishy lips. *Smooch, smooch.* She made kissy sounds.

"Gross!" Stink jumped up and grabbed a toilet brush from the props box. He jabbed it in front of him like a pretend sword. "Back, back, you fiend, or it's Curse of the Toilet Brush for you."

"Guess what? There is *a lot* of kissing in Shakespeare."

"Nah-uh," said Stink. "There's a lot of sword fights and stabbing. Amanda Beth didn't say anything about—"

"Shakespeare's most famous play is *Romeo and Juliet*," said Riley in her know-it-all voice. "Romeo and Juliet are big-time in love. O Romeo, Romeo."

Riley chased after Stink, but he fended her off with the toilet brush. "Death to Smoochy!" yelled Stink.

* * *

Too bad Amanda Beth waited for the end of the day to teach them about Shakespeare insults! "Shakespeare's plays," she told them, "have a lot of colourful words. When a person gets mad or calls someone else a name, the things they say might sound funny to our ears. I'll show you what I mean."

Amanda Beth passed out a list of strange-sounding words. "Use words from each column to make funny-sounding insults. Take these sheets home and practice, because we'll be using our insults later this week."

Spleen face! Canker blossom! Maggot pie! Stink could not wait to try speaking in Shakespeare.

* * *

At home that night, Mum asked, "How was your first day of Shakespeare camp, Stink?" Judy and Dad wanted to hear, too.

"There's good stuff and bad stuff," said Stink. "I learned to make faces." Stink made an I-just-ate-a-worm face.

Stink made an I-just-saw-a-snake face. "And I got to chase a girl with a toilet brush."

"That's good," said Dad. "I guess."

"And today's only Monday. I still get to call somebody a toad-spotted bum bailey and beat somebody up without even hurting them!"

"Let's hear the bad stuff," Judy said. "Was there a lot?"

"No. Just two," said Stink. "Riley and Rottenberger. "

SHAKESPEARE LIVED IN SOME YUCKY TIMES!
IT "STINKS" TO LIVE IN THE 1500s AND 1600s.
P.U.!
A POX ON YOU!
GOT THE PUKES? BLEEDING? PUS-FILLED SCABS? YIKES! YOU'VE GOT THE POX. SMALLPOX, THAT IS. IT MAY HAVE MADE QUEEN ELIZABETH I GO BALD!
BEFORE BAND-AIDS
GOT A CUT? SOAK STALE BREAD IN HOT MILK AND PRESS ONTO THE WOUND. AWAIT THY SCAB!
OUCH!
WHO HAD THE SMELLIEST JOB IN SHAKESPEAREAN ENGLAND? A GONG FARMER, OF COURSE. HE EMPTIED THE PRIVIES AT NIGHT.
A PRIVY IS A TOILET.
PHEW-EE!
SHAKESPEARE LIKED FART JOKES. NO LIE. IN *THE TWO GENTLEMEN OF VERONA*, EVEN THE DOG FARTS! "BUT ALL THE CHAMBER SMELT HIM!" AND IN *KING LEAR*, THERE'S THIS: "BLOW, WINDS, AND CRACK YOUR CHEEKS!"
LOST A TOOTH? NO PROBLEM. IN SHAKESPEARE'S TIME YOU COULD GET A NEW ONE— FROM A DOG, SHEEP, GOAT, OR BABOON!

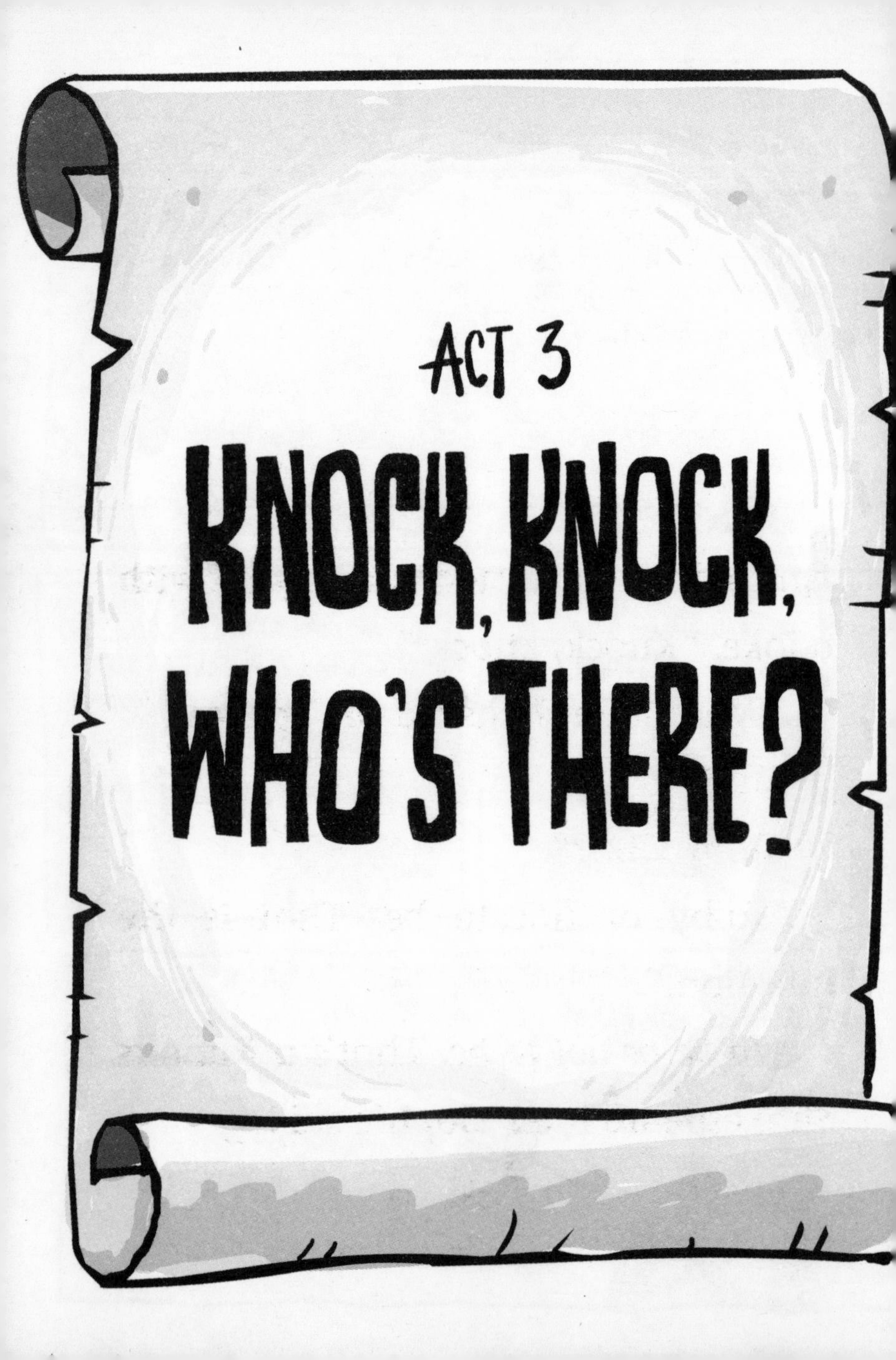
ACT 3
KNOCK, KNOCK, WHO'S THERE?

Amanda Beth started Tuesday off with a joke. "Knock, knock."

"Who's there?" asked the Sprites.

"Toby."

"Toby who?"

"To-by or not to be. That is the question."

"*To be or not to be.* That's a famous Shakespeare line!" Sophie said.

"Good for you," said Amanda Beth. "Did you know we have Shakespeare to thank for the first knock-knock joke?"

"For real?" asked Stink.

"In his play *Macbeth,* you can find the lines 'Knock, knock. Who's there?' when someone knocks on Macbeth's door."

Sophie looked at the Shakespeare quotes on the walls. She made up her own joke.

"Knock, knock."

"Who's there?" asked Stink.

"Arthur."

"Arthur who?"

"Arthur world's a stage. Get it? *All the world's* a stage. It's another famous line."

"Good one!" said Stink. "Knock, knock."

"Who's there?" asked Sophie.

"Hal."

"Hal who?" Riley butted in.

"Hal do I know? I've only been at Shakespeare camp for like a day."

Riley snorted. "You're funny, Stink. I got one. Knock, knock."

"Who's there?" asked Stink.

"Puck."

"Puck's my favourite sprite!" said

Sophie. "From *A Midsummer Night's Dream.*"

"Puck who?" asked Stink.

"Pucker up, Stink." Riley puckered up her lips. *Mwah, mwah.*

"More like *puke,*" Stink teased back.

"Before Shakespeare camp is over," said Riley, "I predict you, Stink E Moody, will be getting a big fat sloppy wet one."

Riley Rottenberger sure had kissing on the brain.

"Remember I told you we'd be doing some fun activities to warm up our voices?" said Amanda Beth. "Let's try some tongue twisters today. Tongue twisters aren't just fun, they help us learn to speak clearly. No need to use indoor voices here. I want your voices to be big and bold. Ready?"

"Ready!"

"Repeat after me," said Amanda Beth. "Red leather, yellow leather."

"Red leather, yellow leather," said the Sprites.

"Smelly shoes and socks shock sisters."

"Smelly shoes and socks shock sisters," said the Sprites.

"Wow. You guys are too good at this. Red blood, blue blood. Three times fast."

"Red blood, blue blood. Red bud, boo bud. Red blue, blood bread."

"Gotcha!" said Amanda Beth, and she chuckled. "Good work. But remember, acting is not just speaking. It's remembering lines, speaking them clearly, using expression, and moving around the stage. You don't want to

be up onstage like this."
Amanda Beth stood stiff as a board, arms at her sides. "It helps to loosen up our muscles before going on. Let's get up and stretch."

Amanda Beth had them reach to the sky, then down to the floor. Amanda Beth had them leap in the air. Amanda Beth had them shake their hands and heads and feet. She even had them stretch their faces by pretending to scream.

"Now we should all be ready to play some acting games. Role-playing is pretending to be somebody else. Think about how a person would feel, what they might say or do. We call this getting into character."

Hazel had to pretend to be an old man and Harper was his new puppy. Sophie and Lily acted like soccer players and Macy was their whistle-blowing coach.

Amanda Beth pointed to Stink and Riley. "Pretend you're in a sweet shop. Riley, you're the mother. Stink, you're the kid, and you want sweets. Go."

STINK: Sweets, sweets, SWEETS! I want sweets. Please, Mummy. Please-please-please-please-please can I?

RILEY: We're not buying any sweets today, Stink. We're just looking.

STINK: Sugar, sugar, sugar!

RILEY: No sugar. Sugar is bad for you.

STINK: Me want gum. Me want lolly. *(Stink popped a pretend lollipop in his mouth and raced around the room).*

RILEY: Stink! No running with a lollipop. You'll fall and get hurt! *(Stink keeps on running).* Come back here, Stink! I'm your mother. You have to listen. Do you want to fall and end up at the hospital again? *(Stink trips and falls).*

STINK: *(on ground, holding knee)* WAAH!

RILEY: Aw, Stink got a boo-boo. Mummy will make your owie better. Where does it hurt? Here. Let Mummy give you a great big—

STINK: Aagh! *(hopping up and running away from Riley)* Never mind, Mummy. I don't need sweets. I'll just have fruit.

TRY THESE TERRIBLY TRICKY TONGUE TWISTERS!
FAT FROGS FLY PAST FAST.
THE SKELETON SLIPPED ON SHAMPOO IN THE SHOWER.
A SKUNK SAT ON A STUMP.
THE SKUNK THOUGHT THE STUMP STUNK.
THE STUMP THOUGHT THE SKUNK STUNK.
WEE WILLY WINKY'S WEDGIE
WAS WORSE
THAN WILLY WONKA'S WEDGIE.

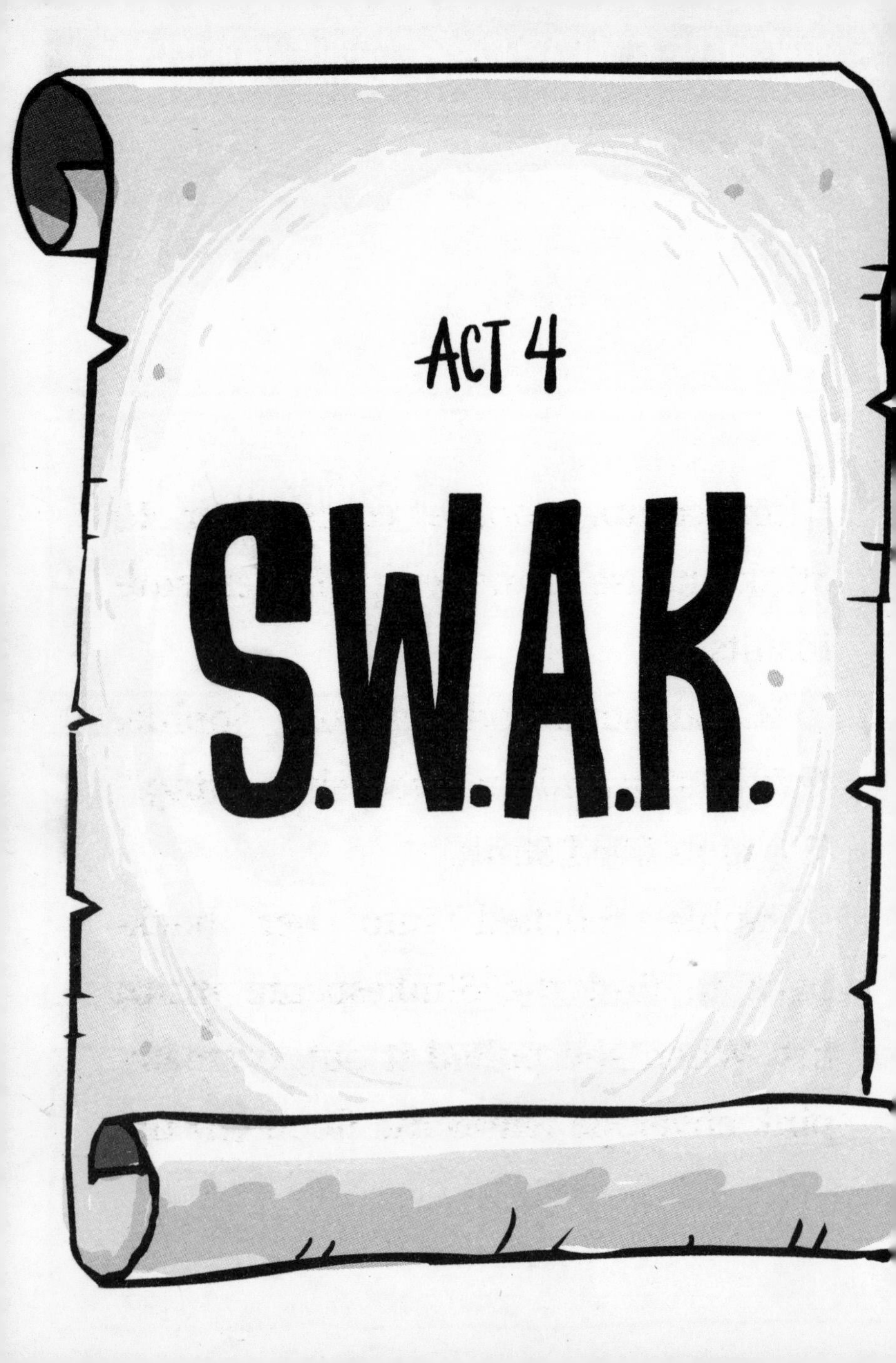
ACT 4
S.W.A.K.

After camp, Sophie came over to Stink's house to make up Shakespeare insults.

"Good save today!" said Sophie. "With Riley and the sweet shop thing." She high-fived Stink.

Sophie reached into her back-pack to find the Shakespeare insult list. When she pulled it out, a smelly pink envelope fell to the floor. On the front of the envelope were the letters *S.W.A.K.*

"What's that?" Stink asked.

"Oh, right. That's a note from You-Know-Who. She asked me to give it to you."

"What's *S.W.A.K.*?" Stink asked.

Sophie shrugged. "Shakespeare Wants A Kazoo?"

"Or Shakespeare Was A Kangaroo?" Stink and Sophie cracked up.

Judy came into Stink's room. "Hi, guys. What's so funny?"

"Nothing. You wouldn't get it," said Stink.

Judy picked up the pink envelope.

"Don't touch that!" said Stink. "It has cooties!"

Judy held it at arm's length. "*S.W.A.K.* Sealed. With. A. Kiss!"

"Gross!" said Stink. "Flush it. Right now. Down the toilet."

"Who's it from?" Judy asked.

"Riley Rottenberger," said Sophie.

"Ooh, a love letter," Judy teased.

"Not funny," said Stink.

"Riley Rottenberger likes Stink," said Sophie.

"Does not," Stink protested.

"Does too. She's Captain Obvious," said Sophie.

"She just thinks she's the best at acting and everything," said Stink.

"She tried to kiss you!" said Sophie. "She thinks she's Juliet. And you're her boyfriend. O Romeo, Romeo."

"Like whoa," said Judy.

"Riley says there's lots of kissing in Shakespeare. Since I'm the only boy, I think I'm gonna get kissed no matter what I do. Methinks I'm going to have to quit Shakespeare camp."

"You can't quit, Stink!" said Sophie. "We didn't even get to sword fighting yet."

"You don't want to miss sword fighting, Stink," said Judy. "I have a better idea. Let's make you an anti-kissing shield!"

"Sweet!" said Sophie of the Elves.

"A shield that's Riley-proof?" asked Stink. "For Riley Rottenberger, you need full body armour. Or a super-atomic, anti-smooching force field wherever you go."

Judy ran to her room and came back with a piece of cardboard almost as tall as Stink. "Here. I was saving this for a good cause."

Stink drew the shape of a shield on the cardboard, and Sophie helped cut it out. Judy got out crayons and markers and glitter and duct tape.

"Let's make a big bad pair of lips with a NO sign crossing it out," said Stink.

Judy drew the lips and Stink and Sophie coloured them red. Stink drew a NO sign over the lips. He duct-taped a handle to the back.

He held the shield out in front of him. "Presenting … the way-official, no-Rottenberger, anti-smooching shield."

"RARE," said Judy.

"Be not afraid of greatness! Some are born great," said Stink.

"And some are born with a great big head," said Judy. She laughed at her own joke and took the art supplies back to her room.

Stink leaped up and tried out the

shield. "Back, back, foul Smooch Monster!"

"Oops. Time for me to go, Stink," said Sophie.

"But what about making up insults?" asked Stink. "I feel one coming on right now. Puke-stocking dung beetle!" Stink cracked up.

"Stink-eyed canker blossom!" Sophie shot back.

S.I.C.K.! (SHAKESPEARE INSULT CREATOR KICKOFF!)
CHOOSE ONE WORD FROM EACH COLUMN. READY, SET, ZING!
VILE
RANK
LUMPISH
GLEEKING
PURPLE
GREASY
REEKY
PEEVISH
PUNY
DANKISH
TOAD-SPOTTED
PUKE-FACED
FAT-KIDNEYED
BOIL-BRAINED
ELF-SKINNED
RUG-HEADED
MILK-LIVERED
ONION-EYED
FLAP-MOUTHED
GUTS-GRIPING
MALTWORM
PIGNUT
CLOTPOLL
HEDGE PIG
DOGFISH
CANKER BLOSSOM
EGG SHELL
FOOT LICKER
MEASLE
RATSBANE
REEKY ONION-EYED MALTWORM
VILE FAT-KIDNEYED HEDGE PIG
RANK TOAD-SPOTTED DOGFISH

ACT 5
The
MACBETH
CURSE

All day at camp on Wednesday, Stink was on the lookout for Smoochy. He kept his shield close, and a backup disguise in his pocket.

At break time, Riley squeezed in next to Stink. *Uh-oh!* Stink had his shield ready, just in case. But then Riley bumped Harper's juice box and it spilled – all over Riley! *Saved by the juice box!*

That afternoon, Stink went down the hall to get a drink of water. Riley Rottenberger followed him.

Stink dashed into the only place where Riley couldn't get to him: the *BOYS'* bathroom. He pulled a fake beard from his pocket. And fake glasses. Ta-da! Shakesbeard to the rescue! Riley would never know him now. *Safe at last.*

Stink made it through the rest of the day – cootie free – by the skin of his teeth.

* * *

That night, Stink put on puffy pumpkin trousers. He put on his WILL POWER T-shirt. He put on a green velvet cape. *Macbeth* time! He forgot all about Smoochy.

Ding-dong! Stink raced downstairs. It was Grandma Lou at the door. And Pugsy! Stink was going to see the play, and Mum and Dad were going out, too, so Grandma Lou was going to stay with Judy.

Stink took a bow. "How now, my fair lady?"

"I fare thee well," said Grandma Lou. "Where's Judy, pray tell?"

"Thy wench be up yonder stairs."

"What wicked tongue have you, young sir!" Grandma Lou teased. "I'm thinking I'll take Judy and Pugsy over to see the play tonight, too. *Macbeth* is my favourite."

"Pugsy is going? Cool!" said Stink.

Grandma Lou slipped Stink some bone-shaped dog treats, and Stink fed one to him. "Holy Hamlet!" said Stink. "Thou hast the breath of seven garlic eaters, Pugs."

Honk! A car pulled up. "Sophie's here," said Stink. He stuffed the extra dog treats in his pocket for later.

"Parting is such sweet sorrow, Pugs. See you at the play!"

* * *

At the far end of the open, grassy area of the college's main quad, a stage had been set up. People sat on blankets and had picnics, waiting for the show to start. Stink and the Shakespeare Sprites followed Amanda Beth around back to a large white tent where the props were stored and where the actors got ready.

"Knock, knock," said Amanda Beth, pretending the tent flap was a door.

"Who's there?" An actor with a fake

beard and a fake belly stuck his head out. "You must be the Shakespeare Sprites," he said. "I'm Ryan." Ryan held the tent flap open so the Sprites could step inside.

The tent was crowded with rolling racks of gowns and robes. Tables were covered with armour, bloody daggers, and a fake head. Stink stepped over a dead-tree prop and snaked around a tray full of plastic turkey legs.

"Welcome, Sprites. As I said, I'm Ryan, and I play the lead."

"You're Macbeth?" asked Stink.

Ryan's eyes grew big as marbles.

WILL POWER

"Uh-oh! It's bad luck to say *that word* before the play."

"What word? *Macbeth*?" asked Stink.

"He said it again!" said Riley.

"We call it the Scottish Play," said Ryan, "or MacBee. We *never* say the name of this play."

"Why not?" asked Stink.

"For the same reason you would never wish an actor good luck," said Amanda Beth.

"Huh? You wouldn't?"

"In the theatre world, it's bad luck if you wish somebody good luck. Instead you say *Break a leg.*"

"Backwards," said Stink.

"Way back when," Ryan said, "the very first time this play was ever staged, the boy playing the part of Lady MacBee got a fever and died. Ever since then, they say the play is cursed. And it does seem like a lot of disasters happen whenever the Scottish Play is staged: storms and fires and accidents on opening night."

"Uh-oh!" said Harper.

Behind Ryan, a man in a crown and a fur-lined cape began to sob and wipe his eyes.

"Why is that guy crying?" asked Sophie.

"Is he crying because Stink cursed the play?" asked Riley.

"That's Mick. He plays Duncan. He's just warming up. That's his way of getting ready to go onstage."

One actor whooped like a monkey. Lady MacBee sang her lines in a high, squeaky opera voice. Somebody else recited the alphabet backwards.

"Do you all know the story of tonight's play?" Ryan asked.

"Amanda Beth told us," said Hazel.

"Yeah, this guy, Macbeth—" *Oops!* Stink clapped a hand over his mouth. He said the *M* word *again*! Stink started over. "The main guy, *MacBee,* wants to be king so bad," said Stink.

"So they have a sleepover, and MacBee kills King Duncan while he's snoring," said Sophie.

"Then Lady MacBee pretends MacBee didn't kill the king," said Riley.

"But MacBee's best friend knows he did," said Harper.

"Amanda Beth told us there are three witches in the play, too," said Sophie. "And they eat eyes of newts and toads of frogs."

"I'll let you in on a secret," said Ryan. "The eyes of newts are just raisins. And the *toes* of frogs are grapes."

Ryan took the Sprites on a quick

tour. They got to try on armour, read a letter to Lady Macbeth, and test out the blood-squirting knife.

Stink lifted up Macbeth's head. "Is this you?"

"Not all of me, but yes. That's me after I get my head chopped off," said Ryan.

"Sweet!" said Stink.

"It's almost showtime," said Ryan. "Better go take your places outside."

"Break a leg," said Stink. "A turkey leg!"

* * *

The Sprites got to sit on blankets right up front. Stink waved to Grandma Lou and Judy, who were sitting on lawn chairs at the back with Pugsy.

It started to get dark outside. Torches flickered inside Macbeth's castle, and the play began.

The play was spooky and not boring. Stink and Sophie sat up on their knees and leaned forward.

"Will all great Neptune's ocean wash this blood clean from my hand?" Macbeth said after killing Duncan. Stink leaned so close that he could see Macbeth's spit fly!

The scene switched to the inside of a dark cave. Shadows swirled around three witches. A large pot bubbled and boiled. Thunder rumbled. *Spooky!*

"Double, double toil and trouble,
Fire burn, and cauldron bubble."

Riley Rottenberger scooted closer to Stink. She looked a little scared. But what if it was a trick, a way to move in close and give him a big fat smooch-a-roo?

A shiver ran up the back of Stink's neck.

"Eye of newt and toe of frog,

Wool of bat and tongue of dog."

The audience started to laugh. *Wait. Why were they laughing?* The scene was super-spooky, not funny.

Then he saw it. *Holy eyeballs!* Pugsy!

Pugsy was on the loose. He ran in circles around blankets, sniffed picnic baskets and leaped over legs. His leash slapped and flapped behind him. *For the love of Pluto!* Pugsy was headed straight for the stage.

"By the pricking of my thumbs,

Something wicked this way comes.

Open, locks, whoever knocks."

Macbeth came bursting out from behind a curtain. "How now, you secret, black and midnight hags?"

And that's when disaster struck. Pugsy raced up the side steps and onto the stage!

Macbeth stopped speaking and the witches stopped witching. Pugsy barked and yapped and ran in circles. He nipped at the hems of the witches' skirts, making them hop and jump in a funny dance.

It was all Stink's fault. He had cursed the play by saying the bad-luck word, the *M* word! He sprinted up the side steps after Pugsy. If only Stink had… Wait! He did! Stink pulled a bone-shaped dog treat from his pocket. "Here, boy. Here, Pugs. Good Pugsy."

It worked! Pugsy came bounding toward Stink. Then, all of a sudden, he stopped. He lifted one leg.

No-o-o!

Stink scooped Pugsy up and turned him to face the audience. "To pee, or not to pee; that is the question."

The audience laughed and laughed. Stink had Pugsy take a bow, then ran offstage with the dog, calling, "The show must go on!"

The rest of the play was perfect. No mistakes. Nobody forgot a line. Nobody tripped and fell. And no more dogs ran onstage!

So the play wasn't cursed after all. Stink had saved the day. And saved the play.

DID YOU KNOW?
WE WOULDN'T HAVE PUPPY DOGS WITHOUT SHAKESPEARE!
HERE ARE SOME MORE WORDS SHAKESPEARE MADE UP. NO LIE!
PUPPY DOG
ARCHVILLAIN
LONELY
SKIM MILK
0% SKIM MILK
HOBNOB
GLOOMY
BUZZER
BEEP!
WILD-GOOSE CHASE
???

ACT 6
POOL NOODLES and PUKEY PICKLES

The next morning, Stink wolfed his waffle in four bites.

"What's the big hurry?" Dad asked.

"At camp today, we get to fight! Two actors from *Macbeth* are coming to show us how. Don't worry. It's not real. In acting, you get to fake fight. You make it look real, but nobody gets hurt. Here, I'll show you."

Stink pulled Judy up out of her seat. He stuck out his arm. "Stand one arm's length apart. Now pretend to hit me—"

"For real?" said Judy.

"I said *pretend.* Act like you're going to slap me in the face."

"No problem," said Judy, grinning.

Judy reached out to slap Stink. He quickly jerked his head to the side and made a slapping sound by clapping his own hands together.

"Pretty neat," said Dad.

"I have to admit, it looked real," said Mum.

SMACK!
#1 DAD
MAPLE

"It sounded real, too," said Judy. "No lie."

"After today, I'll be able to pretend-punch you in the stomach," said Stink.

"Now I wish I was going to that camp, too," said Judy.

"On Saturday we're acting out scenes from Shakespeare," said Stink. "Families can watch, even sisters. It's free, even though in Shakespeare's time it cost a penny."

"RARE!" said Judy.

"Guess what the best part is? I get to drink poison and die!" Stink fell to the floor, then rolled around like he was in agony.

"You'd make a good Romeo," said Mum, "after he drinks his poison."

Gulp!

* * *

When Stink and Sophie got to camp on Thursday, two of the actors from *Macbeth* were pulling pool noodles out of a tall cardboard box in the closet.

"Hey, Ryan!" said Stink and Sophie.

"What, ho! If it isn't the Curse of Macbeth himself!" Ryan teased.

"Yeah. Sorry about the dog running up onstage and everything."

"Oh, that was nothing. One time Macduff was supposed to hold up my head to show that he killed me. But they couldn't find the fake head, so he had to use a basketball. True story."

Stink cracked up. Sophie peered at the other actor. "Hey! You're Lady Macbeth!"

The actor waved a little wave. "Hi, I'm Ryan."

"Wait. *So* you're *Girl* Ryan and he's *Boy* Ryan?" Stink asked.

"That's right." Girl Ryan held up a pool noodle. "How do you like our swords?"

"Very cool!" said Stink.

Amanda Beth started off the morning. "In Shakespeare's time, sword fights were part of everyday life. If somebody didn't like you, say they called you a liar, you might challenge them to a duel."

"A duel is when two people fight with swords," said Riley.

"That's right," said Amanda Beth.

Boy Ryan and Girl Ryan talked about safety first. "No hitting on the head. No getting near the eyes. If one of you calls 'Stop!' the other has to stop."

"Put up thy swords!" said Girl Ryan.

Sophie picked up a purple pool noodle. "Meet the Unicorn Horn."

Stink sat on a lime-green one. "My sword will be called El Stabbo."

Riley held up a red one. "El *Kisso,*" she said.

El Yikes-o!

Boy Ryan and Girl Ryan stood at arm's length and made eye contact.

Girl Ryan taught them how to thrust, lunge and fend off. Boy Ryan showed them how to turn, duck and reverse.

"Don't forget to fake out your enemy." Boy Ryan pretended to crouch down but thrust his sword high over his head. "Fake low and go high."

"Now it's your turn," Girl Ryan told

the campers. "Pick a partner to practice swordplay, one-on-one."

"I call Stink!" said Sophie of the Elves.

"I call Stink!" said Harper and Hazel.

"I call Stink!" said Riley.

Boy Ryan raised his eyebrows and turned to the girls. "You do know this short guy be cursed, right?"

Everybody giggled.

"Let's let Stink choose," said Amanda Beth. "But before you begin your swordplay, I want you to get psyched up. Start by calling out some of those Shakespeare insults we've been learning."

"That'll get the blood boiling," said Girl Ryan.

Hark! Did she say insults? Stink was good at that. "I call Riley!" he blurted.

"Stink!" whispered Sophie. "Are you cuckoo?"

"But I've been storing up pukey words," he whispered back. "This is my chance to let them loose on You-Know-Who."

"Let's say whoever taps the other on the shoulder first wins," said Boy

Ryan. "May the best gentleman, or lady, win!"

Stink and Riley stood at arm's length. "Thou art more loathsome than a toad," Riley started.

Stink swished and swooped his pool noodle through the air. *Shoop-shoop!* "Thou art more pukey than a pickle." Stink did not mean to say pickle. He meant to say something worse. *Slime. Pukenstein.* Anything.

"Beslubbering urchin-snouted mould warp," said Riley. Help! Riley was way-good at this. Suddenly, Stink could not think.

"Brain-sick love worm!" *Love! Why had he said love? What was wrong with his brain today?*

"You yellow-bellied hugger-mugger!" said Riley.

"Milk ... lily ... hedgehog!" said Stink. Something was not right. Something was wrong. Stink could not think of any pukey words. He could not even think of any gross or smelly stuff.

"Hedgehogs aren't gross," said Riley, giggling. "They're cute!"

Fie on thee! Shoop, shoop.

Riley tried to jab Stink in the stomach. Stink groaned and staggered backwards. Fake-out time. Instead of falling, he swung his pool noodle over his shoulder.

Riley did not see it coming. He brought the pool noodle down and tapped her lightly on each shoulder. "Tag. You're dead!"

Riley made a face. She knew she was done for. She crumpled to the ground. Riley was not getting up.

"El Stabbo rules!" cried Stink.

Boy Ryan and Girl Ryan clapped. "Excellent footwork!" said Girl Ryan.

"Good fake out," said Boy Ryan.

Stink leaned over to check that Riley was really dead. Wait just a Macbeth minute. Her eyes were wide open. Just then, Riley reached up and…

Oh, no! What was he thinking? Where was his anti-kissing shield now?

Before Stink could jump away, Riley pulled on Stink's nose. "Got your nose!" she said, making her thumb stick up between two fingers.

Stink turned fifty shades of red. At least Riley seemed to have forgotten about lip-locking.

For now.

STINKO and RILEY-ET
BY STINK E. MOODY
In fair Stink-Upon-Avon, boy meets girl.
IS THAT BEARD A FAKE OR WHAT?
ALLOW ME TO PULL THINE HAIR.
STINKO, O STINKO. LET'S SMOOCH!
ARE YOU CUCKOO? I AM A MOODY. YOU ARE A ROTTENBERGER. ENEMIES. WE SHALL NEVER BE FRIENDS!
FORGET THEM. LET US RAISE SLIME MOULD TOGETHER.
ALAS, I CANNOT! I BE OFF TO SAVETH THE PLANET PLUTO.
MY HERO!
tinko and Riley-et agree to meet at the hark sleepover.
WHEREFORE ART THOU, STINKO?
HERE AM I. WHASSUP?
I AM MAD FOR YOU, STINKO. KISS ME! WHAT SAY YOU?
NEVER! GIRL COOTIES! RATHER I KISS A SHARK!
WOE IS ME, FAIR STINKO! KISS ME BEFORE I KICKETH THE BUCKET, OR I FEAR YOU'LL TURNETH INTO A FROG.
HOW NOW! I'D SOONER BE A FROG... ANY DAY!
Ribbet!
THE END

ACT 7
HAMLET
and
CHEESE

Stink's time had come. Time to shuffle off this mortal coil. Time to croak. As in die.

On the last day of Shakespeare camp, that is, the day before they would perform for their families!

"Great swordplay yesterday, Sprites," said Amanda Beth. "This morning we'll work on what to do *after* the sword fight. We are going to learn how to die a glorious death, just like in Mr Shakespeare's plays."

A murmur of excitement went through the group.

"There are lots of different ways to die in Shakespeare. Let's say poison is poured into your ear while you're sleeping," Amanda Beth said. "Grab your neck like this, stick out your tongue and pretend you're choking. If you're stabbed with a dagger, clutch your stomach, stagger and—"

"Fall on your rear!" said Riley, acting it out.

"Perfect," said Amanda Beth. "And if someone throws a deadly snake at you?"

"Run!" said Harper and Hazel.

"Don't forget to scream," said Sophie.

"Everybody on your feet," said Amanda Beth. "Let's try it."

Riley grabbed her neck and stuck out her tongue. Sophie let out a bloodcurdling scream.

Stink held up a pretend sword and chased after some Sprites. *Swing, swing, stab, stab. AAAAH!* Stink's air-sword was faster than a flying karate chop.

Sprites swooned. Sprites groaned. Sprites crumpled at the knees. Sprites were falling down all around him and calling out, "O, I am slain!"

Wait till I tell Webster about this! thought Stink.

For the rest of the day, the Sprites practiced their Shakespeare scenes in small groups.

"Will you be ready for the Big Wet One tomorrow?" Riley asked Stink. "The Smooch? The Smackeroo?"

Stink tried to scare off Riley with stinky stuff from Shakespeare's time. "I have the pox, you know," he warned.

"Do not," said Riley.

"Then I have the scurvy."

"Nah-uh."

"The vermin?" Stink scratched his head.

"No way do you have lice, Stink."

"BO?"

"No go."

"Forget it," said Stink. "There's no kissing in *Hamlet* anyway."

"We'll see about that," said Riley.

Fie on thee, fly-faced maggot pie!

"Methinks she's mad," said Stink.

"Most true, most true," said Sophie.

* * *

The new morn came. 'Twas Saturday, hither at last! Stink sat in the back seat on the way to Shakespeare camp with his family.

"Tell us about *Hamlet,* Stink," Dad said, talking to the rearview mirror.

"Yeah, let's hear about your big death scene," said Judy.

"Okay. So. There's this king, Claudius," said Stink. "He's the bad guy and he's way into poison. He gets this guy Laertes to fight Hamlet, but Hamlet doesn't know the sword has a poison tip."

"Yikes," said Judy. "Sounds bad."

"*And* ... the bad king says he's

putting a pearl in Hamlet's cup, but it's really a poison pill. Then Hamlet's mother drinks it by mistake!"

"Even badder," said Judy.

"Now comes the sword fight," said Stink, waving his hands in the air. "Laertes gets Hamlet with the poison sword, but in the fight, the swords get mixed up. So Hamlet picks up the wrong sword and kills Laertes with the poison sword!"

"Whoa. What happens next? What happens next?" asked Judy.

"Laertes tells Hamlet that it was Claudius who was behind all this. So

Hamlet kills the bad king. And that's not even the end!" said Stink. "You'll see."

* * *

The stage was set. The time was at last upon yon Sprites.

The Sprites and their families piled into the practice stage room. It had black walls and a black floor. Families sat on raised benches around the room.

"Welcome, friends all!" Amanda Beth announced. "Thank you for coming to our camp. We've had a great week. Today the Shakespeare Sprites will be acting out scenes from several different plays for you. We hope you enjoy the show."

First up were Hazel, Lily, and Jasmine, who acted out a scene from *The Tempest.* There was a storm and a shipwreck. Enter Alonso, Sebastian and Antonio. The three searched the island to look for Alonso's son, the prince. *My son is lost … what strange fish hath made his meal on thee?*

In the next scene, Riley stood on her head and did a backflip, pretending to be Puck in *A Midsummer Night's Dream. Lord, what fools these mortals be!*

"C'mon, Ham," said Sophie. "Our turn." Stink and Sophie stood in front of the audience. They motioned for Harper to come up front with them.

"Hi. I'm Hamlet," Stink said to the audience. "But you can call me Ham. We will be doing the last scene in *Hamlet:* I have just been stabbed with a poison sword by Laertes and am about to die. But I still want to kill my enemy, King Claudius, before I do."

"And I'm the soon-to-be-dead King Claudius," said Harper.

"Greetings," said Sophie, taking a bow. "I'm Horatio, Ham's best friend," said Sophie.

Stink grabbed his stomach, making faces and tummy-ache sounds. He limped across the room with one eye closed, moaning like he was in pain. "Then, venom, to thy work!" he cried. Then, *Swing, swing, stab, stab.* Stink pretended to kill the bad king. Harper crumpled to the floor and closed her eyes. She let her head roll to the side, then made her tongue hang out.

Now it was time for Hamlet to die. Stink doubled over, then fell to his knees. He crawled across the floor, gasping for air. Collapsing to the ground, he coughed, choked and took his last dying breath.

Then Horatio (Sophie) picked up the poison cup. If his best friend was

dying, Horatio wanted to die, too. But Hamlet (Stink), who wasn't totally dead yet, stopped his friend. He convinced Horatio that he must live to tell Hamlet's story. Then he fell back, dead, for real. *Good night, sweet prince. And flights of angels sing thee to thy rest.*

Stink kept his eyes closed and let the mood hang in the air. The audience was dead quiet. At last, he opened one eye to peek. And who should he see, but...

Riley Rottenberger!

By Jupiter! Would she, could she be ... *NOOOOO!*

Riley's warning rattled in Stink's brain. *Before Shakespeare camp is over, I predict you, Stink E Moody, will be getting a big fat sloppy wet one.*

The audience was clapping. Stink's eyes popped open. He leaped to his feet. Sophie took a bow. Stink was supposed to bow, too. Instead, he spun around, looking to make a fast getaway. *Where oh where was his anti-kissing shield when he needed it?*

He felt dizzy. *Why was the room spinning?*

Then, just like that – *smackeroo!* – it happened. The thing he'd feared all week. A Big Fat Wet One. A peck. A smooch. A yucky, blucky, sloppy, slobbery kissaroo. Right smack-dab in the middle of his face.

"BLUCK!" yelled Stink, like he had just smelled a corpse flower.

"Honey? What's wrong?" asked Mum. "I just wanted to tell you what a great job you did."

"We're proud of you, kiddo," said Dad, ruffling Stink's hair.

"You have to teach me how to die like that," said Judy.

Stink hardly heard a word. He turned to Mum. "It was just you?"

"It was just me, what?" asked Mum.

"*You* kissed me. It wasn't girl germs?"

"Just Mum germs," said Mum, laughing. Stink was weak with relief.

He let out a breath. “For a second there, I thought a pox of girl cooties was upon me.”

“Speaking of cooties, Riley’s been waiting for you,” Judy told him.

Stink grabbed his anti-kissing shield and held it out in front of him. “Away with thee, Scurvy Face!”

Riley pulled her hand out from behind her back and leaned forwards.

"No-o-o!" cried Stink, waving his shield like a madman in front of her.

Riley held out her hand with her thumb sticking up between two fingers. "Here's your nose back, Stink."

"My, um, what? Oh, yeah." Stink pretended to take his nose back. "Thanks."

"It's kind of a joke between Stink and me," Riley told the Moodys.

Girls. Who knew? Maybe Riley Rottenberger didn't have cooties after all.

Riley pointed to Stink's face. "You have lipstick on you, Stink. Didn't I tell

you before camp was over you'd get a big fat wet one?" She grinned.

"Thou jesting monkey," said Stink.

"Picture time," said Dad. Stink squeezed between Sophie and Riley, posing for the camera.

"Say cheese," said Mum.

"*Ham* and cheese," said Sophie.

Stink smiled a gigantic smile. "Hamlet and cheese!" said Stink.

What a day. What a way to end Shakespeare camp.

To think! Stink had saved a play and won a sword fight and died a most glorious death. He had been stabbed, poisoned, murdered, and yes, kissed, all in one week.

Shakespeare camp was pure puke-faced fun.

All's well that ends well.

Think you know Stink?

Turn over to find out more!

Check out

Stink's first

adventure!

Meet Stink, Judy Moody's little "bother," er, brother. Very little brother...

Stink was short. Short, shorter, shortest. Stink was an inchworm. Short as a ... stinkbug!

Stink was the shortest one in the Moody family (except for Mouse, the cat). The shortest second-grader in Class 2D. Probably the shortest human being in the whole world, *including Alaska and Hawaii.* Stink was one whole head shorter than his sister, Judy Moody. Every morning he made Judy measure him. And every morning it was the same.

One metre, twelve centimetres tall.

Shrimpsville.

Excerpt from *Stink: The Incredible Shrinking Kid*

COLLECT ALL THE STINK BOOKS!

6
Stink
and the
Ultimate
Thumb-Wrestling
Smackdown
Megan McDonald illustrated by Peter H. Reynolds
7
Stink
and the
Midnight
Zombie
Walk
Megan McDonald illustrated by Peter H. Reynolds
8
Stink
and the
Freaky
Frog Freakout
Megan McDonald illustrated by Peter H. Reynolds
9
Stink
and the Shark
Sleepover
Megan McDonald illustrated by Peter H. Reynolds
10
Stink
and the
Attack of the
Slime Mould
Megan McDonald illustrated by Peter H. Reynolds
11
Stink
Hamlet
and Cheese
Megan McDonald illustrated by Peter H. Reynolds

STINK,
THE WALKING ENCYCLOPEDIA,
HAS COLLECTED SOME OF HIS FAVOURITE FREAKY FACTS INTO TWO COOL VOLUMES.

Stink Moody has his own website!

(One he doesn't have to share with his bossy older sister, Judy)

for the latest in all things Stink, visit

www.stinkmoody.com

where you can:

- Test your Stink knowledge with an IQ quiz
- Write and illustrate your own comic strip
- Create your own guinea pig: choose its colours, name it and e-mail it to a friend!
- Guess Stink's middle name
- Learn way-not-boring stuff about Megan McDonald and Peter H. Reynolds
- Read the Stink-y fact of the week!

IN THE MOOD FOR STINK'S OLDER SISTER JUDY MOODY? THEN TRY THESE

MEGAN McDONALD
illustrated by Peter H. Reynolds
JUDY MOODY
AROUND THE WORLD IN 8 1/2 DAYS
Ciao!
MOOD-TASTIC STICKERS INSIDE
MEGAN McDONALD
illustrated by Peter H. Reynolds
JUDY MOODY
GOES TO COLLEGE
Genius!
MOOD-TASTIC STICKERS INSIDE
MEGAN McDONALD
illustrated by Peter H. Reynolds
JUDY MOODY
GIRL DETECTIVE
Crumbs!
MOOD-TASTIC STICKERS INSIDE
MEGAN McDONALD
illustrated by Peter H. Reynolds
JUDY MOODY
AND THE NOT BUMMER SUMMER
BIG FOOT CLUB
MOOD-TASTIC STICKERS INSIDE
MEGAN McDONALD
illustrated by Peter H. Reynolds
JUDY MOODY
AND THE BAD LUCK CHARM
Whoa!
MOOD-TASTIC STICKERS INSIDE
MEGAN McDONALD
illustrated by Peter H. Reynolds
JUDY MOODY
MOOD MARTIAN
Loop-de-loop!
MOOD-TASTIC STICKERS INSIDE
MEGAN McDONALD
illustrated by Peter H. Reynolds
JUDY MOODY
AND THE BUCKET LIST
1-2-3, wheee!
MOOD-TASTIC STICKERS INSIDE

JUDY MOODY AND STINK ARE STARRING TOGETHER!

In full colour!